TILTING AT WINDMILLS

A MONSTER MARSHALS PAST STORY

TROY LAMBERT

BERT BOOKS

CONTENTS

PROLOGUE: THE PLAIN TRUTH

lains of Spain, 1599

Pablo had been a farmer on the plains of Spain, where much of the rain in the country fell, for nearly two decades, most his life since he had graduated from boyhood to manhood. The ritual to do so had been nearly as brutal as this evening, the woman he'd been offered as large as the harvest moon, the air hot and full of moisture, and his body sweating in terror.

Post-dusk was the best time of the day. The air was the coolest it would be, and clouds overhead promised some relief from the humidity. Pablo grabbed a shovel and walked toward a pile of dung his neighbor, a pig farmer, had dropped off earlier today. It stunk, but there was no better fertilizer.

A movement from behind him and to his left caught his eye, and he spun around to see what it might be. His eyes widened as he saw a ball of fire falling from the sky. The already warm night air got hotter and an odd whooshing sound increased in volume as the object approached the ground. It did not fall like a normal ball of anything would, but instead seemed to level out, like a bird coming in for a landing, and it executed a sharp right turn before settling behind his barn with a crash.

Pablo hesitated. He could run back into his home, but the thing, whatever it was, would still be waiting whenever he came back outside.

Carefully, he walked around the building and could not believe what he saw. It looked like an odd—windmill. Dust blew against his skin. An odd mechanical sound came from within- the creaking and groaning of metal on metal. Three arms extended from the front of it and spun in a circle.

The arms turned in the opposite direction of the wind. As Pablo stepped away from the side of the building, the windmill seemed to rotate so the "arms" faced him. A long, narrow tube slowly appeared and extended from the central hub where they were attached to the structure.

A beam of light shot from it, and Pablo jumped to one side. He felt something odd in the air next to him, a feeling he got when lightning struck close by, and the temperature rose another five degrees in an instant. The grass where he had been standing caught fire.

A new whirring sound came from the thing in front of him, and it rose from the ground, three cylinders that looked like legs bearing it aloft. When the body of the windmill was about eight feet in the air, the whirring stopped.

One of the leg-like cylinders rose and stepped forward. The odd windmill had legs, and its legs had knees, and it was walking.

Pablo screamed. He turned and ran back toward his home, but then changed his mind. To his left was a horse feeding trough. As he leapt inside, several splinters from the rough wood tore into his skin. He held perfectly still.

From outside the trough, he heard the strangest sequence of sounds he had ever heard.

Whir-Thump
Whir-Thump
Whir-Thump

A shadow covered the moon for a moment, and he looked up. The windmill was walking quickly by. Almost running.

Pablo closed his eyes and prayed. Prayed to Jesus, the Holy Virgin Mary, and under his breath swore eternal allegiance to the Pope and the Holy Catholic Church if only God would spare his life.

The *Whir-Thump* sounds got more distant, and soon he couldn't hear them at all.

He needed to warn someone. Scrambling from the trough, he saw what looked like footprints, except that instead of the rough soles of boots, the prints were round, nearly four feet in diameter, and smooth on the bottom.

He ran the opposite direction of the way he thought the windmill had gone with no real idea where he was going at first.

Then it came to him, and he changed direction slightly to intersect with the main road that led into the village. The church would be his first stop.

WINDMILLS?

*V*atican Basement, 1599

"Don Quixote? Are you kidding me?"

"Would you rather use your own name, Mr. Quixana?" Gunther Liefson III had a thick German accent and a nonexistent sense of humor. He was clearly a well-muscled man under the auburn silk shirt and dark jacket he wore. A hat sat perched upon his head even inside his office, and Alonso guessed from its roundness and his lack of facial hair that he was bald.

"What, exactly, am I fighting again?" Alonso looked around the ornate room, as if the answers would lie in the intricate carvings that framed the ceiling, or the paintings of voluptuous cherubs hanging on the walls. There were thin windows at the top of them that let more light into the room than seemed possible. The room smelled somewhat musty, like the dusty pages of old books.

"Martians."

"Martians? What are Martians?"

"Beings from the planet Mars." The German did not smile, and Alonso did not believe he could tell a joke anyway, especially one this elaborate. His hands were folded on a huge expanse of wood. The chair he sat in was covered in an odd green fabric and had wooden arms that matched the color of the desk.

"Planet what? Do explain."

"I think Galileo can do a better job." The German gestured, and Alonso heard footsteps coming down the marbled tile floor of the hallway.

He turned and a relatively young, tall man walked through the doorway. The opening was topped with an intricate cortication, one featuring Adam touching the finger of God. He'd seen a painting like it somewhere before.

The gentleman's hair was graying in stark contrast to smooth skin of his face, and he frowned. He wore the long, dark cloak of an academic with a red silk scarf tossed around his neck.

"Alonso, Galileo. Galileo, Alonso."

"The Galileo? Aw, hell no!"

"There is no proof of the existence of hell. However, I have proof of the existence of other planets."

"Aren't you the round earth guy?"

"Of course. I have proof of that as well."

"Lord Liefson, are you kidding me? Next you will tell me that the god Uranus is in cahoots with Mars, and Mercury quickly sent you a message--"

"Does he think this is a joke?" Galileo roared. "This is not a joke. Other planets are real. The world is round. And Spain is being invaded!"

"Spain. Philip the II, the great incompetent one, is being invaded?"

"Not by the English or some other earthly nations. The Martians!" Galileo stomped his foot. "Lord Liefson, we are wasting time."

"Both of you sit down and shut up!" A vein stood out on

the face of the German, and his fists made balls the size of lion paws. Galileo and Alonso both complied, finding themselves in uncomfortable cold stone seats with high, stiff backs.

"Here is the assignment, Mr. Quixana," the German continued. "You have a choice though. The arena awaits if you do not wish to travel to Spain."

"That was not part of the deal when I joined this team."

"Ah, but it was." The German leaned across the shining wooden desk in front of him. "Do I need to remind you of the contract you signed?"

Alonso sighed. "Fine, what am I up against?"

"Galileo, explain?" the German growled, and leaned back as the astronomer once again took the lead.

"The creatures are from Mars. I am certain of it. I saw some arrive via my telescope."

"Telescope?"

"Through a lens I use to stare at the sky. It does not matter what it is or how it works. That it does is all you need to know.'

"Fine," Alonso stated. "So, I am going to Spain to fight creatures from another planet, Mars, you say?"

"Yes."

"What do these Martians look like?"

"They look a lot like—windmills," Galileo said. "Three big arms in the front. The survivor who saw them described a tube that comes out of the front that shot heat and fire."

"How is a windmill a threat?"

"After it landed behind this man's barn, it walked away."

"A walking windmill? You can't be serious."

"I am serious, Mr. Quixana." Galileo stared at him. "Make no mistake. If the Martians find Spain easy to conquer, the rest of the world will follow."

"So, are you going with me then, Galileo? To help me defeat these creatures from another planet?"

"Nein!" the German answered. "Enough information for now. It is time for action. Galileo will not be going with you. You will take Sancho Panza. He is the best qualified and well versed in the local language."

"Great. The peasant. Just what I needed. I am sure he will be great in combat situations."

"You'll make do."

"Well, where is he?"

"Next floor down, with Francisco."

"There's another floor below us?"

"Yes. The weapons room. Mr. Melzi is very creative."

"Okay, great. I'll get going then. Goodbye, Galil—" Alonso looked around, but the astronomer was nowhere to be found.

* * *

ALONSO PUSHED OPEN the rough stone door. This level of the basement was quite spartan compared to the floor above. The floors were as rough as the door, and not polished or shiny at all.

"Who are you?" a white-robed mountain of a man asked. His graying beard reached nearly to where Alonso assumed his navel would be. It was hard to tell from the gelatinous mound that was his belly. He stood behind a stone table on which there were several deadly looking metal weapons, the likes of which he had never seen.

"Alonso Quixana," he replied. "Agent of the Monster Marshalls."

"Marshalls? I see. They told me to expect someone else."

"Someone else?"

"Perhaps your given pseudonym?" a voice said from behind him.

"Sancho Panza," Alonso said as he turned. "I would say it is good to see you, but it isn't."

"Then the pleasure is all mine," said Sancho.

"Him I was expecting," the large man said. "What is your name again?"

"Quixote," Alonso answered. "Don Quixote."

"Good, *that* is who I was expecting."

"And you are?" Alonso asked.

"He's the infamous Francisco Melzi, the third," Sancho answered.

"I can answer for myself, peasant." Francisco said. "But the low-life speaks truly. I understand you are going to face the tripods."

"Tripods?"

"The Martians."

"You mean the walking windmills?"

"Whatever you choose to call them. We assume they will be weak from the underside, where the legs attach. There has to be an opening for them there."

"We? Who is this we?"

"Galileo and I. We can only make assumptions from the crude drawings we have received."

"Certainly. What else would we do but assume and send the peasant and I in to do the dirty work. And if you are wrong?"

"Then hopefully the weapons I have fashioned for you will still be of some use. If not, I suppose you will die," Francisco stated.

"I'm violently opposed to death," Sancho said. Alonso had forgotten about his presence.

"So are most of the living," Francisco said. "A truly irrelevant observation."

"What do you have for me?" Alonso asked, trying to get the conversation back on track.

"Here," Francesco said, gesturing at the table. "These are a few of my latest inventions."

Alonso picked up a large crossbow-like weapon. On the end were several round objects that looked like simple bronze balls. Several strings were stretched between the arms of the bow portion. "What is this?"

"I call it a repeating catapult."

"What are these?" he asked, pointing at the balls.

"They are filled with gunpowder and equipped with a flint. When they strike something, they explode."

"Explode enough to damage a windmill?"

"I hope so. It seems you will be field testing them soon."

"Hope is a fragile thing. What else?"

"This is a more traditional long bow, with some special arrows."

"Special arrows?"

"They also explode on impact."

"You seem to have a penchant for explosives. That doesn't seem that special."

"Of course not, fool. You see this pod on the end of the arrow?"

"Yes?" Alonso saw something but wasn't clear what a pod actually was.

"It gives the arrow a boost. Light this little fuse as you launch it, and it will fly farther and faster and have more impact than any standard arrow."

"Clever. What's this?" Alonso pointed to a normal-looking lance laying on the table.

"Ah, that is my latest experiment. It is a lance that will launch from the handle and shoot like a firework into whatever you aim it at."

"A firework, huh? Okay. How do you aim it?"

"Point and shoot like this," Francisco said, and grabbed the weapon. He spun, faster than Alonso assumed his bulk would allow, and stuck his arm straight out. He twisted his wrist, and the tip of the lance flew toward a stone wall a mere fifteen feet away. It embedded itself in the brick with a bang and stone and dust rained down around them. Alonso fell to the floor and found himself staring into the terrified eyes of Sancho.

"What was that?" the peasant asked.

"Either a great mistake, or our salvation," Alonso muttered, and stood to his feet. The dust was still swirling, and the lance quivered in the opposite wall.

"Oops," Francisco said with a shrug. "At least, you know it works."

"Do you have more?"

"I have four—" Francisco stopped and tilted his head. "I have three to send with you on your journey."

"Good," Alonso replied. "I like your lance a lot."

"Good to hear. Best of luck to you."

"Thanks," Alonso said, turning to Sancho. "I'll grab one lance and the cross-bow. You grab the extra lances and the sack of exploding balls."

"Okay," Sancho said. "But that ball sack looks heavy."

"You can manage," he told the peasant. "How are we getting there anyway?" Alonso turned and asked Francisco.

"I nearly forgot!" the inventor said. "You'll be taking the helicopter."

"The what?"

"Da Vinci never perfected it, but I have. You, gentleman, will take the first helicopter flight across the Mediterranean Sea."

"Flying?"

"Yes, come with me, and I will give you a quick lesson."

Alonso grabbed the handle of one lance in his left hand,

and the cross-bow type device in the other. Behind him, he heard the clank of Sancho picking up the other two lances, and the clang of bronze as he lifted the sack of balls over his shoulder.

It had already been a day of unbelievables. Why would they not be flying to Spain in a strange, untested craft?

2

SPAIN

The boat rocked as they drifted toward the shore. The helicopter had not worked at all, not boosting Alonso's confidence in the rest of their equipment. Francisco had muttered something about not accounting for the weight of his armor, but there was no way Alonso was going without it. So, they had taken passage on a frigate carrying freight, and then disembarked with a small dinghy to reach the shore. Alonso rowed, Sancho watched.

On the ship, the peasant had chattered incessantly about nothing, but as they made their way toward the beach ahead, he got eerily quiet. Now, he sat perfectly still, eyes wide, a terrified expression on his face.

"Cat got your tongue?" Alonso asked as they reached a stone pier stretching out from the white sand. He smelled an odd mix of salt water and grime.

"What?" Sancho answered. "No. I mean, I am just thinking. I look forward to our adventure."

"Sure you do," Alonso replied, racking the oars and climbing to the bow, where he uncoiled a rope and looped it around a piling. "C'mon, then. Let's get on with it."

"Don't forget your name," Sancho said, handing him the crossbow, the lance, and then the bag with the extra lances and balls.

"My name?"

"Your pseudonym."

"Of course not." Alonso scoffed and set everything on the pier. "Let's go find some transportation."

It was a short walk to the market and a longer walk to the stables. The stalls looked strangely empty.

"Good morning!" Alonso shouted.

"Not so loud!" came a shrill voice from the depths of the shadows. The place smelled of hay and fresh horse dung, two of Alonso's least favorite odors.

The owner of the voice appeared to be an impossible man who had not reached five feet tall but was nearly that around. He somehow managed to walk on two stumps that served as his legs. They appeared to have knees, and on what should be feet, he wore tiny little boots that could not possibly support his bulk. He wore black trousers and a shirt that had once been white but was now decorated with brown and yellow stains. A top hat of sorts was perched atop his head intended to make him appear taller, but instead enhanced how small he really was.

He stopped and stared. "What's with the armor?" he asked.

"I am a knight, on a noble quest," Alonso answered.

The short man bowed, if that was possible, an awkward gesture that seemed like it might end in disaster. "They call me Gary Hertz. I am master of these stables. How may I serve you?"

"Gary? That is an unusual name."

"My parents are emigrants to this land. What are you called, Sir Knight?"

"Quixote. Don Quixote. We require two your finest stallions."

"Oh, that is quite unfortunate."

"Why is that?"

"There is a convention in town, and they have overrun us with requests."

"Indeed? The place looks rather empty. What do you have left?"

"I'm embarrassed to say, but come this way Mr. Quixote, and your squire?"

"Sancho," Sancho answered.

"Yes, Sancho and Don, do follow me."

The man led them down a narrow aisle. On either side were empty stables, some with tack still hanging on the walls, some completely bare. Flies buzzed, and it was warm although the sun did not reach the interior of the building. Ahead, Alonso heard braying.

Braying?

"Here we are," said Gary. He gestured to his right.

In the stall were two rather large donkeys, mules perhaps. Both had long, ridiculous ears, and black manes on dark gray bodies. They looked strong, but not fast.

"This is it?" Alonso asked.

"I am afraid so. They are sturdy beasts. Perhaps they will do for your quest?"

"Is there another stable in town?"

"No, sadly that enterprise went out of business."

"Then I suppose we have no choice."

It took them longer than Alonso would have preferred to get the mules ready. Both were sturdy but stubborn, and Sancho was, well, Sancho.

"Let's get going," Alonso said. "I'd like to reach the village before nightfall."

Sancho mounted his steed, and the two walked toward

the edge of town. The armor earned him a few looks, some snickers and smiles hidden behind hands.

They were almost to the main road when a female voice came from behind them.

"Nice ass," the voice said. "Where are you going dressed like that?"

The source of the voice turned out to be gorgeous. She had the dark, curly locks of the women of this land, but they were red rather than brown or black. The woman was heavy in both hips and breasts, the latter of which were displayed prominently. Her cleavage was a Grand Canyon, so deep a river might hide within it.

"Who—" Alonso's voice squeaked at the word, and he cleared his throat and started over. "Who might you be, M'lady?"

She sat upon a stallion that immediately made him jealous, first because he would have loved to be astride the stallion rather than the mule he was on, in the second place because he would have liked to take the horse's current position.

"I am Dorotea, but you may call me Dora. You are new here? What is your name?"

"Quixote. Don Quixote," Alonso answered, proud of himself for remembering to introduce himself properly. "My squire, Sancho, and I are on a noble quest."

"I am sure. What knight does not have a quest that is noble? What is this 'noble' quest?"

"We are going to help the peasants of a village called La Mancha to defend their homes."

"La Mancha?" she looked puzzled. "What possible threat could there be in that tame countryside?"

"Walking windmills!" Sancho suddenly blurted, and Alonso stared at him. "I mean—" Sancho stopped talking and hung his head.

"Walking windmills? You believe the nonsense Pablo was spouting?"

"We have been hired to check it out," Alonso said. "I'm certainly not yet convinced."

"Well, Sir Quixote," Dora said. "Good luck to you and yours. May the saints shine upon your journey."

"May I ask what brings you to this fine town before we take our leave?" Alonso asked.

"My father, Samuel de Champlain, is here for the explorers' convention," she said. "Good day, gentlemen."

Alonso watched as Dora turned to ride away and saw that she wore a square pack strapped to her back.

"How odd," he said. "And you, Sancho?"

"Yes, My Lord?"

"Keep your mouth shut. Now, let's go. On to La Mancha!"

As they rode out of town, he had the odd feeling they were being watched.

3

LA MANCHA

La Mancha, 1599

They approached what was supposed to be a village as a slow drizzle of rain fell. It was not quite enough to drench them, yet not light enough that they or their possessions would dry out anytime soon.

The streets, if they could be called that, were well worn paths just wide enough for two horses (or mules) to walk down side by side. Scattered throughout the area, some near the "streets" and some far from them were scattered homes. Some had thatched roofs made of prairie grass.

Others were made of some kind of wood. These roofs appeared sturdier than the rest, some with stone chimneys rising from the interiors. Small wisps of smoke came from a few, and the smell of alder smoke rose on the evening air. The journey had taken much longer than they had expected. There had been a lot of traffic headed the other direction, carts filled with possessions or families, headed toward the bigger towns.

He could not tell if these were peasants fleeing their homes, or people headed to some kind of weekend market.

Alonso had no idea what day it was. Certainly, Sancho would —the peasant had little on his mind, but Alonso would certainly not stoop to asking him.

The streets were oddly empty, the shops closed up for the night. A larger stone building at the end of the street bore a giant wooden sign, and as they approached, Alonso read the words "Inn and Tavern."

"Perfect," he said, turning to Sancho. "I could use a good night's rest."

"Me, too," Sancho said. "All this riding has made me quite parched."

"We've talked about this. We are on a mission. No excessive drinking."

"Si," the peasant said sadly. "Nothing to excess."

"You do not sound convincing."

"I will temper myself," Sancho replied. He looked away, but Alonso had no energy to argue or to worry about it.

The check-in process had been simple, although the stable hand had looked at them sideways as he took their mules. There were plenty of rooms, they learned. The innkeeper complained that business was down due to much of the population being out of town, and a new service called Breeze B &B, something Alonso had never heard of.

Once they put their things in the rooms they had been assigned, they went downstairs to the tavern.

Through the odd set of doors, they could hear a band playing loudly. Guitars, drums, and a tambourine kept a steady rhythm. As they entered the room, the music stopped. Those who were dancing paused, and all eyes were on them.

The silence stretched from one minute into two as Alonso and Sancho made their way through the crowd to the bar. As soon as he held up two fingers, the music and the dancing resumed.

A darker ale than he was used to appeared on the bar in front of him. "What's this?" he asked the bartender.

"It's a local brew called Alhambra," he said. "Taste it."

Alonso took a sip. "Not bad," he said. "You brew this here?"

"Of course. Tell me, *amigo*, what is with the armor?"

"My squire and I are here on a noble quest."

"A noble quest? In La Mancha?"

"To find and stop the walking windmills!" Sancho exclaimed again.

The music and dancing stopped once again. Every eye in the place was on them, save one. It belonged to the bartender, who had one lazy eye clearly not focusing on anything at all.

"You're here to what?"

"We've been sent to check out the reports of some strange happenings here," Alonso replied, glancing at Sancho and shaking his head.

"Sent by whom?" The bartender seemed to speak for everyone, but there was a hint of hostile menace in the atmosphere. "And what is your name?"

"Quixote. Don Quixote. And I have been sent from the Vatican itself."

"You represent the church?"

It wasn't strictly true, but Alonso did not wish to know what would happen if he denied it. "Yes," he said.

"Good," he said, and waved his hands. "May I talk to you in private, My Lord?"

Alonso simply nodded and followed when the bartender gestured to a side room.

As he looked back, he saw Sancho had finished his beer and was already on a second. The insistent hand of the bartender on his elbow kept him from going back and offering a warning.

"A confession? I am not a priest!"

"But you are from the church?" the bartender pleaded.

"Yes, but not a priest."

"Still, surely you can hear my confession?"

"I can hear it," Alonso answered. "I am not sure I can do anything about it."

"I will do penance, My Lord."

"What if I do not know what penance to offer you?"

"It matters not," the bartender replied. "It will sooth my soul either way."

Alonso sighed. He was not sure what to do. To refuse might foil their chances of discovering any information here. To give in—who knows what one might hear in a place like this.

"I can offer you information," the bartender said. "About some strange happenings."

"For example?"

The bartender looked around as if making sure no one was within earshot. "The walking windmills—I have seen them."

"You have seen them?" Alonso asked.

"Yes. Those your squire spoke of. They are the—strange happenings you are here to investigate, yes?"

"Something like that. Tell me what you saw."

"It looked, well, sort of like a windmill. The blades—they were arms. Three of them. Then the—thing—rose up on three legs."

"Three legs?" Alonso asked.

"With round feet," the bartender whispered. "It walked right toward me, but I hid."

"How many others have seen these?"

"Only a few of us. At least, those that will talk about it. Others—well, I am sure they have seen them. They are just afraid to talk about them."

"That's understandable. It sounds — crazy."

The bartender recoiled. "Mr. Quixote! I am not crazy!"

"I never said you were," Alonso reassured him. "I said it sounded crazy."

"Now will you hear my confession?"

"What? That wasn't it?" Alonso asked.

"N-n-no," the bartender stammered. "That was just the information I have for you."

"Okay. I will hear it," Alonso said. "What is your confession?"

"Father," the bartender kneeled. "There is no proper confession booth here, but it has been nearly a year since my last confession."

"Is this going to take long?"

"No, Father," the bartender said, head bowed. "It is just these feelings I have been having for my sister, Isa—"

The sound of shattering glass interrupted his words.

Alonso stood. "Maybe I will hear more later. Until then, you are absolved and all that."

"Um, sure," the bartender stood. "But what penance—"

More glass shattered, and Alonso fled toward the other room, the bartender right behind him.

Sancho stood on the bar, dancing. Apparently, he had kicked two glasses off the bar in the process, and three men were trying to coax him down.

The band had stopped playing, but Sancho was singing anyway:

"And it's just like the ocean under the moon, oh, it's the same as the emotion that I get from you…"

The lyrics went on, and they would have been catchy except for Sancho's poor voice. The song did not sound Italian or particularly Spanish in origin.

"Sancho!" Alonso yelled. "Get down!"

The peasant yelled something in Spanish that Alonso did

not understand, apparently a curse, because a large man snarled and grabbed his leg, pulling him from the bar. The smell of the local beer filled the room as another glass shattered.

Alonso rushed forward as the man grabbed Sancho by the collar and raised his fist.

A cold breeze blew into the bar just as Alonso grabbed his arm, and everyone paused and turned to look. A tall woman with a shock of dark red hair walked through the door.

"Pedro, put that man down!" she commanded. "Or I shall never grace this bar with my presence again."

The man complied, and Sancho fell to the floor with a thump. Alonso rushed to his side.

"Lo siento, Dora," the man said with a deep, rumbling voice. "May I buy you a drink?"

"No, I want to buy her drink!" another voice said.

"Please, Dora, allow me!" said another.

"It is my turn to buy her first drink!" said another. "You can buy for her later."

Alonso looked up from Sancho's drunk but whole form to see a scuffle breaking out between the four men. One was slapping at the others, keeping them back. Pedro, the big man who had grabbed Sancho, clenched and unclenched his fists, circling the slapper in the center.

"Boys!" Dora yelled. "No fighting!"

The bar quieted once more, and every man leaned forward as if to hear her next words.

"Pedro will buy my first drink, and one for my friends," she gestured to Alonso and the now snoring Sancho. "The rest of you can buy the next rounds, si?"

"Si!" came the shout from the crowd. The band started to play once again.

"Come with me, Don Quixote," Dora motioned. Alonso awkwardly pulled Sancho from the floor, half-carried, half-walked him to the table, and tossed him in a chair which rapidly overbalanced and fell, resulting in the peasant's head striking the floor with a hollow thud.

Alonso was unsure if that was because the area under the floorboard was hollow, or because there was nothing in the peasant's skull worth speaking of. He suspected the latter but picked him up and balanced him in the chair anyway.

"Sorry about that," Alonso mumbled. "Hi again."

"What happened?" she gestured at the peasant.

"I left him alone for a moment. Clearly a mistake in a bar, but the bartender…"

"The bartender what?"

"He heard I was from the church and wanted to make a confession."

"A confession? But you're not…"

"I know. I am not a priest, but he insisted."

"Whatever did he confess?" Dora leaned forward, her elbow on the table, fist under her chin.

Alonso found the pose adorable. "He has seen the… he had some information about our quest."

"He's seen the walking windmills?"

"Yes, the very ones the other peasant claims to have seen."

"Pablo is no peasant. He is a prominent farmer, well respected."

"My apologies."

"None needed. You are not noble yourself, Quixote?"

"Touché," Alonso said. "So, why are you here?"

"To help you, of course."

"Help us what?"

"Help you track the windmills."

"You think twenty-foot-tall, three-legged windmills walking around will be hard to track?"

"Yes. I think they will hide in plain sight."

"Fair enough," Alonso said. "I have no plan besides gathering information first. I suppose you have one?"

"Of course," she said. "What weapons do you and your..." Dora trailed off and indicated Sancho. "… squire have with you?"

A round of three drinks arrived with the bartender. "Sorry to interrupt, my Lord. But the rest of my confession?"

"I am sure what you are feeling is very natural. Go in peace. I absolve you, my son."

"My penance?"

"Ten 'Hail Mary's' and we will forget we ever spoke of it."

The bartender wandered off, muttering. Alonso put both his and Sancho's beer in front of himself. "We have a few interesting devices," he said, and explained to Dora what information he had and what they had been given to fight the Martians. Through most of the explanation, she just nodded, asking few questions.

She proceeded to outline a plan, and Alonso liked it, all but the role she had for Sancho. He did not think the peasant was nearly reliable enough to carry out that mission.

4

AND THEN THERE WERE WINDMILLS

"Are these the balls?" Dora asked, indicating the sack over Sancho's shoulder.

The peasant seemed chipper, probably because he had slept through much of the discussion in the bar. Alonso's head hurt, the bright sun sending stabs of pain into his eyes, and his mouth was dry. Inside the ridiculous armor he was sweating buckets, so much he feared the moisture would rust the joints and he wouldn't be able to move.

"Yes, they are," he answered.

"They feel heavy," she said, picking up the bottom of the sack.

"I'm sure once we shoot off a few, the sack will get lighter," he said. "The peasant is strong. He can carry them all day."

Sancho just grinned.

"Let's get going," she said. "Before it gets any hotter or starts to rain."

"It is humid," Alonso said. "But rain, today?" He gestured at the cloudless blue skies.

"It may be clear now, but really, it can storm here anytime," she said. "These plains are where most of the—"

"I've heard," he said, cutting her off. "Let's go."

He and Sancho mounted their mules, splitting the weapons between the two. Dora, of course, mounted her gorgeous stallion.

A gorgeous woman on a gorgeous stallion, and here he was, a fool on an ass. What could she possibly think of him?

As they started to ride though, he kept catching her glancing at him. They talked along the way, her of Spain and he mostly listening.

Even though the temperature rose, he didn't feel it as much as he thought he would. The armor was heavy and hot, but he was adjusting. Sancho took the lead, riding casually. His words would occasionally drift back to them, mostly him singing in Spanish.

Then he stopped. As Dora and Alonso pulled up alongside him, he pointed.

"Windmill," he said. About a quarter of a mile away, a windmill stood in the center of a field. It did not look like it belonged there, but rather as if it had been tossed randomly into a field of crops. It straddled the rows diagonal to their pattern.

Its arms seemed oddly thin for a windmill, but they turned slowly. Still, there was something wrong with the way they spun.

"Backwards," was the only other word Sancho said.

"It's one of them," Alonso said. "Give me the repeating catapult!"

Sancho pulled it from its place on the back of his saddle and handed it over. Alonso dismounted and took the rest of the weapons off the back of his mule. "I will leave these here to save some weight. Except for the lance. I am taking one of those."

"Remember, there are only three, My Lord," said the peasant, the first full sentence he had uttered since his song the night before.

"I know," Alonso said. "I plan to use the balls if at all possible." He checked to find the catapult fully loaded. "Give me a couple extra, just in case."

He put the extras in a small pouch on his belt.

Alonso exhaled sharply. "Here goes nothing," he said.

"Oh, for the love, Quixote!" Dora said. "You're just tilting at windmills. Get on with it already."

The mule moved forward at a steady trot. Alonso wanted to go faster, but on the other hand, he didn't. Just tilting at windmills, indeed. Giant, people-crushing windmills from another planet made that sentence a little different.

As he rode toward the windmill, the wind shifted and so did the arms, moving in the opposite direction.

Odd, he thought. *These beings must be truly intelligent.*

Alonso scanned the ground for the odd round footprints he had been told about but did not see any.

Nor was there any of the burnt oil smell he had been told to expect.

Nothing.

This building looked like a regular windmill. Yes, the arms were different. The closer he got, the more doubt he had.

Then he saw it. Behind the arms, the windmill moved. Not the arms, but the building itself, almost as if it would lift off the ground.

Thinking better of his options, Alonso clipped the catapult to his belt and raised the lance instead.

"You there!" he yelled. "What are you?"

The building shuddered but did not rise on three legs. It just sat there.

Could his eyes—

Then the arms of the windmill stopped moving. He could feel that the wind was still blowing. One arm seemed to reach for him.

Alonso kicked his mule into a charge, which in this animal's case was more like a lope, lance forward. He saw movement behind the now still arms, and twisted his hand as he had been shown, firing the explosive lance. It flew true to his aim, and stuck where the arms attached to the windmill, exploding.

A shower of wood flew from the building, splinters bouncing off his armor.

Wood?

One of the arms fell forward, landing with a thud in the field.

Splinters?

"What the hell are you doing?" a voice yelled. It came from the direction of the windmill and took the shape of a man. He stood about ten feet in front of the building, covered in sawdust.

Alonso reined in his mule. "I'm sorry, I thought…"

"You thought what?"

"I thought your windmill was…"

"Was what? I just finished fixing it. I put a new brake on the arms so I could keep it from turning too fast in a storm. Why did you… what did you do to it?"

"I… listen, I can explain."

"I am waiting!"

"Come along now, Donnie," Dora said. He hadn't noticed her ride up, but her stallion was suddenly beside his mule. "*Lo siento, mi amigo,*" she said. "This is my brother Donnie, and he is special."

"Donnie?" the farmer asked.

"Well, Quixote actually. Don Quixote. He thought your windmill was another knight."

"Another knight? It doesn't look a thing like a knight!"

"I know, and I am sorry. Listen, I am from the Vatican—"

"You don't look like a nun," the man interrupted.

"You could say I kicked the habit. It's too hard to explain. I'll just take my brother now. Contact your local parish, and they will pay for the damages."

"Okay. Who cares about the pay? Who will do the work?"

"We'll send him back later," said Dora, pointing to Sancho. "For now, we need to get moving."

"How do I know I can trust you?" the man said.

Dora just stared at him, and eventually he dropped his gaze to the tops of his work boots.

"We'll talk later," she said. "Go on about your business."

"Yes, My Lady," he said.

As they turned and rode off, Alonso remained silent. The whole thing was embarrassing. He'd fired on a real windmill. He's actually killed a real windmill with one of their few lances.

"Only two now," said Sancho.

"It's okay," Dora said quietly. "You okay, Mr. Quixote?"

"Not really," Alonso said. "I feel pretty silly."

"As you should. It did look unusual."

"So you say."

"And you were brave, even if…"

Alonso looked over at her to see why she had stopped speaking and saw that she was holding back laughter behind her hand.

"What is so funny?"

"Ah, Dios. Cost of that lance? Who knows? Rent on the mule? Seven pesetas a day. Seeing you riding on that loping mule charging that windmill? Priceless!" She stopped her horse under a small tree, the only tree they had seen for a long time and doubled up in laughter.

"Hilarious!" he said. "When did you realize it was not one of the aliens? Why did you not stop me?"

"To achieve success, one must first fail many times," said Sancho with a chuckle.

"You stay out of this peasant!" Alonso exclaimed. "The two of you having fun at my expense is fine. Wasting our weapons is not."

Sancho had now dismounted and was laughing at least as hard as Dora.

Alonso looked from one to the other. "Are you quite finished?"

"Not quite," said Dora. "Brave Don Quixote slays windmill," she said, moving her hands through the air as though framing a headline or a giant sign. "News at 11!"

Sancho laughed even harder. Alonso stepped from his mule to the ground and tied him up.

"Hilarious, you two," he said, and leaned against the tree. He pictured himself on the mule. Pictured himself charging an actual windmill.

He could see the movement in his mind's eye now, see that it was the man coming out of the windmill to admire his braking work. He could see how normal it had all looked.

Until he had shattered it with an explosive lance.

Alonso started to laugh, too. It was a little chuckle at first, but the more he thought about the situation, the funnier it seemed. His gut shook with laughter. The harder he laughed, the harder the others laughed. Sancho fell over, rolling on the ground.

Alonso's eyes blurred with tears. He'd killed a windmill. A real, honest to God and the Saints, windmill.

Then he stopped. Clouds were building on the horizon, but there was something else. Closer to the ground. A mile away, maybe less, there was movement. A very tall windmill, walking on three legs.

From the middle of where the arms attached to the body, a light struck out in a beam and a barn just in front of it caught on fire.

Looking at the walking thing now, even from this distance, he didn't understand how he could have mistaken an actual windmill for one of these.

"Look!" he said.

"Sure," Dora said. "Do you see another one?"

Alonso grabbed her arm probably a little rougher than he should have and spun her around.

"Look, damn it!"

She did. Her mouth opened and closed in surprise as her laughter stopped mid-chuckle.

Even Sancho stopped laughing and looked in wonder.

"What do we do now?" he asked.

Dora shook loose of his grip. "We see if your boss can use his balls this time," she said.

"I can," Alonso said, suddenly filled with adrenaline and courage.

"Good luck," Dora said as he mounted the mule. He held one of the final two lances in his hand, the catapult still attached to his belt, the extra balls still in the pouch hanging there.

"Thanks," he said.

"One more thing, Don Quixote," Dora said.

"Yes?"

"You ever grab my arm like that again, and I will break yours. Hero or no hero."

"Yes, ma'am," Alonso said, facing the walking windmill. He rode forward, feeling rebuked yet strangely aroused.

5

THE REAL THING

The mule charged much faster this time, and Alonso was unsure why. The animal almost seemed to know this was real. Perhaps the beast was more intelligent than he had imagined previously, and had been trying to get him to slow, to look more closely.

Indeed, it seemed possible that ass had been trying in its own small way to keep him from making an ass of himself.

The tripod, as Francisco had called them, if that is what the three-legged monstrosity was, had kept moving across the plain toward a small collection of buildings. One was a barn, and the others seemed to be small houses or cottages except for a larger one off to his left. That one appeared to be a stable.

As the thought crossed his mind, the thing shot another beam from between the three arms that made up its blades. The ground ahead of it caught fire for a moment, and Alonso saw the silhouette of a man running beside the flames. They died quickly, finding no fuel, but the thing was even closer to the buildings now.

From the stable, he heard braying, and understood finally

what the mule he was on might be sensing: there were other mules in the structure, and they were in danger. It was the same thought he was having about the man he had seen and others who might occupy the buildings ahead.

His mule brayed loudly, perhaps answering the calls ahead. Immediately, people began to pour out of the structures. Alonso could now see human shapes pointing and waving. Two ran toward the stable, and a mere moment later there were mules everywhere, fleeing from the thing approaching them.

"Faster!" he called, but his mount needed no encouragement. Alonso was now a windmill slaughtering knight, and he was headed directly into battle. When he was a mere fifty yards away, the creature must have sensed him because it turned. The strong scent of burning oil filed his nostrils.

The mule reared up in a way Alonso had no idea was possible and moved as if it would turn around. Alonso squeezed with his knees and pulled hard on the reins. With a nearly human whine of protest, his mount dropped to all fours and continued forward.

Balancing as well as he could, Alonso aimed the lance, waiting. The center of the three arms glowed red as if the creature were readying another bolt of light. He knew he did not have time. There was no doubt he would not survive a direct blast. He aimed the best he could for the underbelly between the legs because there was a rectangular area that almost looked like a door there. With a twist of his wrist, he fired the lance.

This time it struck home in the center of the door-like area. There was a muffled explosion. A beam of light shot from the center of the spinning arms, but went sideways, missing him by a good thirty feet. Still, the temperature in his armor rose by at least ten degrees. One of the three legs buckled, and the thing started to fall towards him.

Fearing it would crush him, Alonso rode to his right, his mule jumping over a small log, then moving through a pall of smoke. As they emerged, they saw a small group of people standing there, and they all began to clap.

Behind him, he heard a loud crash, and another puff of smoke and dust rose into the air, quickly engulfing them. The mule stopped when it could no longer see.

Alonso slid from its back to the ground, pulling the repeating catapult from his holster. He turned and walked back toward the place where the windmill had fallen. A moment later, he saw its squarish shape, and as the dust settled it became clearer.

Two of the three legs it had been walking on had retracted, leaving only two grass-stained ovals visible, apparently the bottom of its feet. The third leg appeared to be broken near where it would have retracted, and an odd whirring sound came from the place it intersected the body. Small tendrils of acrid gray smoke came from that area, and he smelled burning oil again.

The arms, or blades, whatever they were, had stopped turning or moving at all. When he went around what he assumed the front of it to be, the light between them where the beam came from appeared to be weak, much dimmer than before. As he watched, some odd blue sparks came from it before it disappeared completely.

The magnitude of what he had done suddenly hit him. He had—killed? — whatever this creature was, and he did not even know anything about it. He'd been in danger, perhaps grave danger, and walked away, essentially unscathed. Without thinking, Alonso dropped to his knees and crossed himself, looking at the sky.

The cheers of the people watching woke him from his trance. As did the sound of an approaching mule and a fine stallion.

"Madre de Dios!" Sancho exclaimed. "You actually did it!"

"I had no doubt," said Dora. Her grin made Alonso feel even warmer than he already did inside his heavy armor.

As they rode up, the group of people who had been looking cheering, rushed over. There were at least twenty of them, maybe more. Most shouted and waved their arms, then one man stepped forward.

"To whom do we owe a debt of gratitude?" he asked.

"To this great knight!" Sancho said, gesturing to him.

"And what is your name, good knight?" the man asked.

"Quixote. Don Quixote." Alonso swallowed, hard. His vision blurred, he smelled sulfur, and suddenly he wanted to throw up. Somehow, he threw his hands in the air in a victory salute.

Then he swayed, felt his vision darken, then clear just in time to see that he was falling forward, face first into a pile of donkey shit.

* * *

ALONSO'S NOSE WAS, literally, filled with the smell of donkey dung, a mixture of stomach-processed hay and grass that was less than pleasant. As he sat up, he blew out each nostril, grimacing at the globs of shit that shot from them. Looking up, he saw Dora kneeling beside him.

"Are you okay?" she asked. The crowd has dissipated, apparently disappointed by his display of mortality.

"Yeah, this armor is just warm, I guess."

"Here, drink," she said, offering him a flask.

He took a sip then spit out the foul-tasting liquid. "What's this?"

"Some kind of elixir that's supposed to rehydrate you and make you feel better."

"It tastes a bit like piss," he said. "Can I just have some water?"

"Sure," she said. "It's just that she gave it to me for you." Dora gestured, and he saw a wrinkled, bent woman leaning on a cane a short way off. She wore a gray robe that flowed to the ground, and a hood was drawn up around her head, wisps of graying hair poking out around her face.

A giant nose dominated that space, and when their eyes met, she smiled, or at least intended to. The single tooth dangling from her upper gums made the expression look more like a grimace.

"Is she a witch?" he asked.

"Not sure if that is accurate in the traditional sense. She's a medicine woman, I assume."

"Ah, so she is a witch."

"I would not call her that."

"What would she do? Turn me into a newt?"

"It would prove your point. Still, I would drink the beverage she offered if you can stomach it."

Alonso took the flask back from her reluctantly and, eyes on the medicine woman, raised it to his lips.

Her grin widened if that was possible, and she gestured with her hands for him to go on. Hesitating only for a second, he did.

Once he got past the initial bite, the drink was merely salty, and made him thirstier for water. There was a citrus undertone to it he could not quite identify, along with a strange odor. He did feel better, so he kept drinking.

"This tastes like orange, almost, but like one past its prime."

"She says it is called Goatade and is good for those going into battle."

"Well, thank her for me. Where is Sancho?"

"Tending to the donkeys."

"And the…thing?"

"The villagers carried it off in pieces. Not sure what their motive was."

"I would have liked to study it, see if I could learn more of its weaknesses."

"That would be helpful. Do you want the good news or the bad?"

Alonso sighed. It was always something. "Good, I suppose."

"We know how to kill them, and the lance was very effective. Getting under them seems to be the key, through that odd opening on the bottom."

"The bad news?"

It was Dora's turn to sigh, and then look off toward the mountains north of them. "You have but one lance left. Reports from the villagers say two of the tripods remain, walking and destroying together just north of here. The tripods may force you to battle both at the same time."

"Another reason it would have been good to study the one I killed."

"You will need help, Don Quixote. More help than Sancho can give."

"What do you propose?'

Dora outlined a quick plan, and he simply nodded. Alonso had other ideas but kept them to himself at the moment.

6

ONWARD

The first thing on Dora's agenda, one Alonso would not refuse, was a meal. During that time, he removed the upper part of his armor and let his body air out. They had more of the drink the medicine woman had offered, although she still stood a way off, watching them eat, but not joining them or saying a word.

Sancho rejoined them after seeing to the mules and the single stallion they possessed. The villagers, if that's what they could be called, slowly drifted back and some brought gifts of food.

One brought a sweet-smelling bread, much fluffier than the heavy flour breads he was used to. A spicy sausage of some sort followed, and although it tasted similar to beef, he was reluctant to ask its origin. The same was true of a sour but fragrant cheese almost soft enough to spread on the bread. Everything tasted as good as it smelled.

Sancho must not have noticed the taste, for he pretty much inhaled the food, crumbs flying everywhere. Dora satisfied herself with a single piece of bread folded in half, meat and cheese stuffed in the middle. The effect was a neat, edible package.

"What are you doing?" he asked.

She swallowed a bite she had just taken, wiping cheese from the corners of her mouth. "Creating a popkin."

"A popkin?"

"Yes. A bread package to hold all of my food together. I got the name from a poem or a book I read once," Dora explained.

"Whatever it's called, it's brilliant."

She nodded. "The only thing better would be if the bread came from the baker already sliced."

"At the moment, I can't imagine anything better." Alonso sighed. "Enough loafing. We have a battle ahead."

"We do. You do not wish to rest for the night?"

"The tripeds will merely have time to do more damage in that case."

"Tripeds?"

"Three feet. That is what I have decided to call them."

"Clever, and you are right, of course," Dora answered. "I have one alteration to my plan."

"Yes?"

"I think you should ride the stallion this time."

"Your horse?"

"Yes. You are the heroic knight. You should not be stuck on a mule."

"I'd be honored."

"Good. It is settled. Are you ready, Sancho?"

The peasant nodded, but his face betrayed his doubt.

"Let's go then," Dora said, and Alonso rose to his feet. He did feel much better after drinking the flask of Goatade and looked around for the witch to thank her, but she was gone.

The stallion seemed a bit skittish, but Alonso mounted

him anyway once he had donned his armor again. He carried the final lance and the repeating catapult.

Sancho carried three long lengths of rope, two they had put together with knots from rope they had been carrying the entire trip, the other a continuous length he had discovered in the unburned area of the stable. Since none of the villagers remained, they simply took it with them. This was the part of the plan Alonso was unsure of.

Dora carried the bow with the exploding arrows. She looked decidedly uncomfortable riding his ass, and he almost offered to trade her back. The stubborn and grim look on her face told him that would be a bad idea.

The narrow road led north, and the people they had just rescued gathered in a small group and waved as they rode away. Again, Alonso looked for the old woman among them, but did not find her at all.

No matter, he thought. *We can thank her on our way back.*

The sun left the sky, and the stars and moon came out to replace it. A breeze brought the smell of grasses to his nose, and he swore if he listened hard enough, he could hear it growing. There was no sound but that of their mounts' feet striking the soft trail. None of them spoke.

Tension rode with them. It stayed in the middle, sometimes ahead, sometimes behind, but always between them. The road rose toward what appeared to be a wide pass between two hills, for since he had been brought up near the Alps, he could not think of them as mountains.

Alonso could not see beyond them but assumed the creatures they were to battle would be in the next valley. Up ahead, he saw a bridge, although he was unsure what body of water it might cross.

"There will be monsters," Dora said quietly, pointing to round footprints beside the trail.

"Si," said Sancho.

The trio descended into silence again.

As they approached the bridge, Alonso saw cattle in the draw below it. Some were drinking water from a small and, apparently, seasonal stream there. The rest were grazing on long grasses that grew around it.

The sound of the stallion's hooves on the bridge startled some of them, and they looked up. Ahead, he could see there were more cattle around the pass, many with horns. The smell of cow dung mixed with the fresh grasses, and he found it less unpleasant than he thought. There were now two sets of round footprints, one on either side of the path.

Less than a quarter of a mile past the bridge, they crested the hill. What had probably once been a beautiful valley spread out before them. There was grass, but it was dotted with smoldering fires, some of which had once been structures.

There were cattle everywhere, hundreds of them. Even at this range, he could see where a couple of them had been trampled by the tripeds.

In the distance, there were, indeed, two tripeds chasing the large animals, and he paused for a moment to watch the running of the bulls. Their presence could complicate the plan, but it was too late to rethink things now.

No people were visible, but he was certain they were present somewhere, hiding if they were wise.

If he were wise, he would instruct the two with him to do the same. Suddenly he was weary, the energy sapped from him. His armor felt heavier than it had just moments before. HIs adrenaline felt distant and useless, the sweat on his body his only reality. But he had been tasked with a mission, and he intended to see it through.

He kicked the stallion into a trot, but not a run, and looked to find the others had done the same. The wind whipped around him, and his eyes burned with the smoke. It cleared for a second, revealing an angled path to intercept the first creature. He left the road, riding straight for it.

As he approached, the creature turned as if it had heard him. As it did, the stallion stopped short, and Alonso could not lock his knees in time. He flew over the animal's head, and for the second time found himself face down on the filthy ground.

At first, he thought he landed in mud, but as he sat up to regain his bearings, his sense of both smell and taste also returned. Clearly, this was bullshit.

He looked up just in time to see the stallion running back the way they had come, and a giant, round foot descending toward him.

Alonso rolled, and as he did, saw Sancho riding to his right swinging the end of the long rope like a lasso. Before he knew what had happened, the rope was around his arm and he was being dragged along the ground. The grass was surprisingly slick and smooth. Suddenly, an idea came to him. Twisting his body, he grabbed the rope with both hands and found his footing. Now he was being dragged while standing.

His feet bounced over hidden rocks, but the ground was surprisingly level. Sancho must have spurred his mule to run even faster, because his speed was building and keeping his balance became more challenging. Still, he held on.

"Go around it!" he yelled, and Sancho apparently got the message. Meanwhile, the triped was turning in place trying to watch them. A hay bale loomed ahead, and he flexed his knees and jumped as he got close.

His heavy armor kept him from clearing the obstacle, and his foot clipped the top of it. Managing to still hold on to the rope, he landed on his back, spun his feet once under the rope, and, amazingly, found his them again.

"Let out more rope!" He yelled, but Sancho was thinking

along the same lines. His progress slowed a little, but Sancho got further ahead and then turned in a tight circle around the creature, darting between two of its legs. Alonso slid toward the peasant with every intent of crossing his path. As he did, he braced himself, and loosened the lasso loop around his arm, grabbing it with both hands to keep his balance instead. Ahead, he saw the final lance sticking out of the ground where it had stuck when the stallion threw him.

With one fluid motion he tossed the rope to Sancho, who quickly slid the loop through the other end attached to his saddle. Alonso kept sliding forward, and grabbed the lance, pulling it free of the soft ground. He then dropped onto his back and turned around, pointing the lance at the creature. As he watched, he saw Sancho riding away, rope in tow. It tightened as the creature moved forward, and he heard a large creaking sound.

As Alonso's slide ended, the triped tripped. The knee of one leg buckled, and it fell forward. The ground shook as it struck, and a new burning smell was added to the already smoky air. He heard a metallic scream as a thick beam of light shot from the front of it, scorching the ground, leaving a path of burned destruction in its wake.

The weak underside was only feet away, and Alonso took careful aim, twisted his wrist, and fired the final lance. His arms shook, and he missed. The lance flew past the monster and struck a large cow. It exploded, lighting up the night for just a moment as it caught fire, and illuminated Sancho on the back of a mule riding for his life.

"Now, that's roast beef," he said.

Behind him, he heard the sound of approaching hooves, then felt gravel spray his cheek. An arrow flew from above and behind him, striking directly in the creature's weak underside. A second one followed, and then a third, all on target. They exploded one after the other and, with a metallic roar, the light coming from the triped died.

A second later he felt himself airborne, lifted by the back of his armor, and then he was across a saddle in front of Dora.

"Hang on!" she said and rode into the darkness away from the dying creature.

He wanted to ask questions, but could not, as with every step the wind was knocked out of him. The mule stopped, and he slid to the ground, tripping and landing gracelessly on his side.

Dora descended behind him and helped him to his feet. Another two sets of hooves approached, and Sancho appeared out of the darkness leading the stallion. The peasant was covered in blood as was the mule he rode.

Alonso felt his head spinning, and then nothing.

7

FINAL MOVES

"There's one more triped left."

Alonso tried to sit up but felt nauseated and fell back on his elbows. Sweat pooled in areas where he never knew he had areas, and he wished for another flask of Goatade or just water.

He removed his helmet and tossed it aside. Gingerly, he removed the upper part of his armor, and tried to push out the dent the creature had put there. It didn't work.

His ribs hurt, and he had no idea how they would take care of the last of the tripods.

"The plan is shot," Dora said. "We have no more lances, only a few of these arrows, and two balls."

"Two balls? There were way more in the sack when Sancho took off with them!" Alonso said.

"Yes, but the sack, it spill when you blow up the bull." Alonso could read the frustration on his face through the blood smeared there.

"I didn't mean to blow it up," Alonso said.

"You miss with the last lance, almost kill me."

"You're fine. The triped is dead, isn't it? I'm going to count that as a win."

"No thanks to you. The girl is the one who save us."

"We work as a team," Alonso said.

"The two of you can stop fighting," Dora interjected. "We need to kill the last of the tripeds, and so we need a new plan."

"Like the old one worked?" Alonso said. "We just need to go kill it."

"We will have to find it first."

"Where did it go?"

"It ran off as soon as the other one fell," Dora said. "And now it knows it is being hunted."

"So, it will be ready."

"Si!" said Sancho. "And we did not do so well last time when it did not know we were coming."

"We'll just have to make do. At least, it will not be hard to track," Alonso said.

"What do we have left for weapons?" Dora asked.

"We just covered this," Alonso said. "But—"

"I have two balls," Sancho interjected.

"And the rope," Alonso added. "We still have one of those, right?"

"Si," Sancho said.

"And three exploding arrows," Dora said. "That's what killed the one this time."

"It means no one can miss," Sancho said.

"Funny," said Alonso. He looked down at himself and removed the bottom part of his armor.

"Why are you doing that?" Dora asked.

"It's too hot," Alonso said. "I'm going to face this thing head on."

"Without the cover of knight?" Dora said.

"You think you're funny, but you're not," Alonso said, forcing a smile.

Staggering just a little, he grabbed the repeating catapult and the two balls, and mounted the stallion.

The others climbed onto the mules and as they did, it started to rain.

They rode side by side in silence. The rope was looped between Sancho and Alonso, and Dora carried the three exploding arrows. Not trusting Sancho to carry his balls, Alonso had them between his legs in a sack along with the catapult. Ahead, the creature was moving away from them at a rapid pace.

The ground shook with its steps. No light beam shot from it to destroy anything in its path, but occasionally the giant, round feet would stomp on a cow, eliciting a loud, bellowing cry and leaving a pile of ground beef.

The air smelled of blood, a sticky-sweet odor mixed with the rain falling in a steady drizzle, reminding them of the penalty for failure. A small breeze caused Alonso to shiver, and in the silence, his shudder was almost audible. He almost wished he had his armor on again. No birds sang, no villagers were gathered in groups to cheer them on. It was down to them vs. the triped.

Ahead, a large hill rose toward a snowy peak. Heavy forest lined the rapidly rising ground, and just before the creature reached the trees, it turned. Smart. There was no way to flank it now. They would have to face it head on.

The creature braced its legs, and then a beam of light came from between the three arms on what appeared to be its face.

With no choice, the three split up. Alonso and Sancho went left, Dora to the right. The beam struck the ground where Dora had been, and the air instantly heated.

"Go!" Alonso shouted.

He and Sancho separated, stretching out the rope between them. When it was nearly tight, they rode madly toward the creature, trying to stretch it wide enough to capture two of its legs and trip it.

Before they could get close enough for their plan to work, the creature turned and let loose with the beam once again. This time, it scorched the rope between Alonso and Sancho, immediately burning it to ash and making it worthless. Sancho veered even further left just in time, as a second shot from the creature decimated the spot where he had been a moment before. Alonso rode closer, aiming to get under where the creature could reach him, and raised the catapult. He'd lost track of Dora, and Sancho was riding frantically away.

With as much precision as he could muster with water running into his eyes, Alonso fired. The first ball struck the soft spot under the creature and stuck there but did not explode. Before he could fire again, the creature moved, this time attempting to trample him. Alonso pulled the reins rapidly, steering his horse right just as the large foot slammed into the ground. He felt the wind of it as it narrowly missed him.

Then he saw Dora, bow raised, riding under the creature as well. She aimed and fired, her arrow slamming into the creature and sticking into it right next to the ball. The arrow exploded, but the blast was muffled, and the creature did not even falter.

Instead, it tried to trample her, and Alonso raised the catapult for a quick shot. The ball flew forward and struck the creature's leg, bouncing off and falling onto a patch of soft grass just beyond it.

Dora, too, pulled her mule to the side to avoid the heavy foot, but it reared as she did so, and threw her to the ground.

Alonso had to do something. Dora rose, running toward

the trees, trying to get away from the now dancing feet of the creature. The triped emitted sound like a mechanical roar. It seemed angry.

Spurring his horse, Alonso rode forward, unsure what he was doing. He had no weapons, a short piece of rope, and nothing else. Still, the ball lay on the grass just beyond the creature, unexploded. Dora should have two arrows left, were she given the opportunity to use them.

Then he saw her. Somehow, the witch, or rather the old woman from scene twenty-four was here. She was standing just outside the tree line. As he rode, the witch glided forward to where the ball had landed. She moved more quickly than seemed possible for such a small woman.

Still Dora ran, first one way and then the next, keeping herself from under the feet of the angered creature. The air smelled of burning oil, like a lamp had been left too long and was nearly dry.

Alonso spurred his mount, and then heard an odd, mechanical groaning from his left. He turned and saw Sancho. The peasant had fashioned a lasso of sorts and had it around one of the creature's legs. The other end was attached to his saddle horn, and his mule was pulling for all he was worth, frequently slipping in the muddy earth. The creature stopped stomping around and braced its feet to balance against the new assault.

The witch reached the ball laying on the ground before Alonso did, and as he approached her, she tossed it to him.

Riding with no hands atop his panting stallion, he caught it with one, and loaded the odd catapult in a smooth motion he had not known himself capable of. Turning around, he saw Dora kneeling with the bow, an arrow notched and ready to fire.

Everything moved in slow motion then. He heard a snap from his right and glanced over to see Sancho had just lost the tug of war when the rope broke. The peasant and his mule flew backward, the animal stumbling, Sancho flying from its back and rolling across the ground.

The creature stumbled with the release of the pressure, and all three feet pounded the ground as it attempted to keep its balance. Dora was right in the path of one of them.

Without thinking, Alonso took aim and let the shot fly. The ball struck the creature right next to his previous shot. An arrow appeared between the two balls, indicating Dora had also fired.

The large steel foot was coming down directly over her. Alonso was ten feet away, maybe too far, but he dove from the back of his horse anyway, reaching for her.

Everything happened at once. He grabbed her and rolled her over with his momentum, feeling the heavy foot narrowly miss them. He kept rolling, not knowing where it would land next.

Just then he heard two explosions close together. The mechanical roar came again, the burning oil smell got stronger and mixed with gunpowder, and then the creature started to fall, fortunately away from where Sancho lay, motionless. With a puff of dust, it fell to the ground. Yet, it still appeared not to be dead.

The three arms still moved slowly, and from between them a tube appeared. The legs retracted all the way except for one, and the tripod used it to right itself and aim the strange tube right at them.

Alonso could feel the heat building. In a single motion, he removed the bow from Dora's hands ignoring the pain in his shoulder, grabbed the final arrow, and lit the fuse as he had been shown. With careful aim, he fired it directly at the tube. It flew directly inside and stuck there. The sound and the explosion combined were much larger than what the arrow could have done on its own, and the arms actually flew from the center hub, landing in the grass nearby.

Alonso rolled once again to get away from the flames, but the move was unnecessary. The creature stopped moving.

Somehow Dora had ended up on top of him, and Alonso found himself staring into her eyes.

"You seem to have saved my life, Mr. Quixote."

"You seem to have done the same for me," Alonso replied.

"How ever can I thank you?" she asked.

"I'm sure we can think of something," he said, smiling. She leaned down as if to kiss him, and he closed his eyes.

"Woo Hoo!" he heard, and he felt Dora move before he opened his eyes to see what was happening.

Dora stood, and the peasant was right there, his hand held high. Dora slapped it with her own hand, and they both smiled broadly.

"You are hero!" the peasant exclaimed and offered him his hand. Alonso took it and allowed himself to be pulled to his feet.

"I don't know if I would have been successful if it were not for the witch," he said, looking around for her. As he did, she approached.

Slowly, she removed the scarf over her head, and as she did, the gray hair came with it. She straightened, and Alonso could see that she was actually a he.

"Who are you?" he asked.

"I'm Miguel Cervantes, a scribe of sorts. I was sent along to witness your story so I could write it down."

"What?"

"The German. He wants me to write it so that the people will have an explanation of what happened, at least a story of sorts."

"I never heard of such a thing."

"Probably not. My role is… unusual."

"So, you will write about all of this?" Alonso asked, suddenly wondering if his real name might be used.

Cervantes scoffed. "You mean how it actually happened? No, no one would believe this. No one sane anyway. As far as the world knows, Don Quixote is quite mad, and his sidekick Sancho is simply indulgent of his madness. Tilting at windmills, indeed."

With that, the writer walked away.

"What now?" Dora asked.

"Well, I suppose we must head back to the Vatican at some point to make a report. However, since the scribe seems to be ahead of us, there is no reason we can't delay for at least a little while."

"That's good. We've also got to send Sancho back to repair the first windmill you 'killed.'"

"True. Perhaps there is somewhere I can wait for him while he does his work?"

"There is certainly still some room at the explorers' convention."

"That sounds quite nice," Alonso said.

A look of concern crossed Dora's face. "Oh no!" she said. "I seem to have lost my backpack. Can you help me find my backpack?"

Alonso looked at her and shrugged but she simply kept staring at him in a strange and quite uncomfortable way. He broke eye contact and looked around for the strange bag.

"I found it!" Sancho exclaimed, running over holding the backpack by one strap. "Here it is. Here is the backpack!"

"Good job," said Dora. "You found the backpack!"

Sancho looked pleased and grinned from ear to ear.

She took it from the peasant. "You better get going to repair that windmill," she told him. "Don and I will be along shortly."

The peasant rode away on his donkey, and they were alone. They faced each other, looking into each other's eyes.

"I would like to get to know more about you, Don Quixote."

"I feel the same, Dora, the Explorer."

"Just one thing," she said.

"What would that be?" Alonso asked.

"If we're going to explore each other, you must learn to speak Spanish along with Italian. That is, after all, my native language."

"I've always wanted to learn a new tongue," Alonso said. They kissed, hesitantly, and then more deeply as the rain stopped and the sun rose, creating an orange glow behind them.

THE END

JOIN OUR EMAIL LIST FOR FREE BOOKS, UPDATES AND PRIZES

Did you enjoy this story? If so, I would love it if you could leave a review. It's something authors appreciate more than anything. I hope you are excited for the next chapter in Max's story.

Max's story is just beginning. And there are some other great stories coming soon. The next in the series, *Compelled*, will be coming this fall, and you won't want to miss it.

In a small town in Montana, a woman disappears, and her family suspects the worst.

And a serial killer, silent for three years, starts killing agin. .

Want to keep up with Max and his stories? Want free books and special offers, and starting soon, a free story every month? Subscribe to our newsletter on my website. We'll only send you bargain books and let you know when new stories are coming. You'll never miss a release.

Harvested is also available in audio format! Find it on Audible and other retailers where you listen to audiobooks.

If you want to join our exclusive review team, see our

website for more information. (There is a test, but it's an easy one, I promise!)

In the meantime, be well. More exciting fiction coming soon!

ABOUT THE AUTHOR

Troy Lambert is a full-time writer and author. Having written over two dozen mysteries and other novels, Troy is well-versed in story creation, and he knows what it takes to make a fictional story real! Troy's hobbies and pastimes (when he's able to break away from the computer) include hiking into the mountains of Southwest Idaho, fishing in a fast-rushing stream, and going for a drive where his mind can work on creating that perfect twist to the book he's currently writing. A native of Idaho Falls, Idaho, Troy and his wife live in Meridian, Idaho. You can find his other works, including his latest book, *Teaching Moments*, at troylamber-twrites.com.

ALSO BY TROY LAMBERT

THE MAX BOUCHER SERIES:

Teaching Moments

Harvested

THE SAMUEL ELIJAH JOHNSON SERIES

Redemption

Temptation

Confession

MONSTER MARSHALS

Miner Inconveniences

Tilting at Windmills

NON-FICTION

The Tao of Trek

Writing as a Business: Production, Distribution, and Marketing

7 Steps to Plotting Your Novel Quickly

THE DOG COMPLEX

Stray Ally

"Fast Break"

Book #1 "Overdoses in Olympia"*

Book #2 "Slaying in Salem"*

Book #3 "Strangled in Sacramento"*

Book #4 "deCapitated in Carson City"*

Book #5 "Buried in Boise"*

"The Wicked West"—a compilation of books 1-5, available in both e-books and print*

Book #6 "Hanging in Helena"*

Book #7 "Branded in Bismarck"*

Book #8 "Parricide in Pierre"*

Book #9 "Carnage in Cheyenne"*

Book #10 "Defenestration in Denver"*

"The Nick of Time"—a compilation of books 6-10, available in both e-books and print*

Book #11 "Silenced in Salt Lake"*

Book #12 "Poisoned in Phoenix"*

Book #13 "Stung in Santa Fe"*

Book #14, "Axed in Austin"*

Book #15: "Offered in Oklahoma"*

*These books are now available in audio format!

All the books in the "Capital City Murders" series are available at www.CapitalCityMurders.com and your favorite e-book seller.